Suebrenia Calhoun
Illustrations by Kaila Richman

How Daisy Became the
Luckiest Girl in the World

Bumblebee Books
London

A CIP catalogue record for this title is
available from the British Library.

Scripture quotations are taken from the Holy Bible, New Living
Translation, copyright ©1996, 2004, 2015 by Tyndale House Foundation.
Used by permission of Tyndale House Publishers, Carol Stream, Illinois
60188. All rights reserved.

ISBN: 978-1-83934-075-8

Bumblebee Books is an imprint of
Olympia Publishers.

First Published in 2021

Bumblebee Books
Tallis House
2 Tallis Street
London
EC4Y 0AB

Printed in Great Britain

www.olympiapublishers.com

Dedication

This labor of love is dedicated to
Jesus Christ,
The Giver of good gifts.

Robert,
My husband and life partner for his unending confidence and support of my professional goals and dreams.

Earnestine Hales,
My mother and best friend in heaven who defined love with her life.

Joseph E. Rogers,
My father who gave me the important position of Daddy's Lil Girl.

Daysia, Robert Jr., LeTisha and my grandchildren,
My beautiful family for all your love and support.

Darl Drummond,
My aunt who named me and has always spoken greatness over my life.

My family and friends in Mississippi and Florida,
For whatever part you played on my journey,
Lu2Life, Sue.

To my family who have always supported my art since I was a little girl,
(And my cats who I'm sure would too),
Kaila Richman, Illustrator

Ring! Ring! Bam! Bam! The hallways were filled with screeching sneakers, slamming lockers, and expired inside voices turned up to the highest degree on the last day of school.

"No running, guys!" warned Mr. Lee.

"Yes sir," the boys muttered quietly with a temporary stop from their black and gold basketball high tops.

The summer break had finally arrived at Joseph Edward Elementary School.

"I am so glad I don't have to do homework anymore," said Daisy while gathering all of her self-made lucky charms from the top part of her locker. "Here's my rabbit's foot, my lucky pencil, and my black-and-gold lucky socks. Oh no! Where is my pink good luck bracelet? It was just here a minute ago," Daisy panicked.

"There it is, Daisy. It's behind your P.E. shirt," chuckled Denise blocking the air vents of her nose from the rising stank. "That is the weirdest looking rabbit's foot I have ever seen," said Denise.

"Actually," explained Daisy, "it is a raccoon's foot. My dad is from Georgia and he believes God made animals to be a part of the food chain. When he cuts their feet off, I pray over them and ask God to give me good luck," Daisy said undisturbed. "I have a box full under my bed if you need one," Daisy kindly offered.

"I think I will pass," Denise quickly answered.

"Whew," gasped Daisy. "That was a close one. I thought I lost my magical, lucky bracelet. I'm going to my grandma's house in Mississippi for the summer, and I have to wear my bracelet every day. My cousins and I play kickball, dodge-ball, and my favorite game of all, Red Light, Green Light. When we play Red Light, Green Light, you have to freeze for the red light and run for the green light to the finish line. The first one to make it to the end is the winner. When my big cousin, Danielle, says red light, everyone must stop and stay very still. She gets so close to our face and tries to make us laugh so we can start all over again. And when she talks, little white spit monsters leap into our eyes. If we blink, she makes us go back to the starting line. Wearing my pink lucky bracelet will help me dodge those spit creatures and win every time," explained Daisy.

"That sounds like fun, except for the spit invasion. When I go to my grandmother's house for the summer, she churns the best homemade vanilla ice cream in the world," said Denise.

"Yummy. That sounds delicious, Denise. My Mississippi grandma doesn't like us coming into her kitchen while she is preparing dinner. She lets us walk to Ms. Strickland's store and get my favorite brain-freezing, strawberry-and-grape snowball. I cannot wait," said Daisy.

"You are a very lucky girl, Daisy. Have fun," said Denise as they did their special farewell handshake.

"See you in September," yelled Daisy.

"Good luck!" Denise said.

Daisy's plane was scheduled to leave at 6:30p.m. Her parents picked her up immediately after school.

"Honey, I hope we are not late for the plane," Daisy's mother said to her father. "You should have waited to go fishing tomorrow. The traffic is always heavy this time of the evening," she said with frustration.

"I have to cut the lawn tomorrow, and you know I can't fish on Sundays. I'll catch the devil," Daisy's father said sarcastically.

"Mom, we will get there in time. I am wearing my pink lucky bracelet, and everything will be fine," Daisy assured her mom with a smile.

Daisy and her parents arrived at the airport just in time.

"Flight eleven, eleven is now boarding for Jackson, Mississippi," a perfectly pitched lady voice said from the airport speakers.

Daisy waved goodbye to both of her parents as the tall, caramel skin toned flight attendant walked her to the first seat on the plane.

"Good luck, honey!" her parents echoed.

"Have you ever flown before, Daisy?" asked the flight attendant.

"No, ma'am, but my lucky bracelet is sure to get me there in one piece," said Daisy clasping her fingers around the loosely joined pink balls.

"You are a brave little girl. I will have to buy myself one of those lucky bracelets. Just relax, Daisy, and I'll be right back," the flight attendant said.

"Yes, ma'am," Daisy answered politely.

Before Daisy could finish her honey roasted peanuts and pulp-filled orange juice, the captain announced, "Fasten your seat belts, ladies and gentlemen. We will be landing in fifteen minutes."

"Buckle up, little lady. It is time to land," said the flight attendant.

The waiting area of the airport was crowded with people standing on their tip toes pointing at what seemed to be friends or perhaps family members.

"Daisy! Daisy! There she is, Aunt Stella, holding the tall lady's hand!" shouted Danielle.

The three distant cousins skyrocketed towards each other to begin their long-anticipated reunion.

Daisy turned and yelled, "Goodbye," to the flight attendant.

"Good luck!" the attendant said.

All the way home, Daisy, Danielle, and Monique discussed their summer plans. Their conference meeting was so intense that they did not notice the car parking into grandma's U-shaped driveway.

"Hey look! We're here!" yelled Daisy.

As the girls scurried out of the car, Daisy asked, "Can we play Red Light, Green Light?"

"Yeah," Danielle and Monique sang in harmony!

"Let's start at the end of the driveway and the finish line will be the back of Grandma's car," Danielle, the oldest cousin instructed.

Danielle hollered, "Good luck everybody! On your mark! Get set!"

"Wait!" screamed Daisy. "Where is my pink lucky bracelet?" She whimpered with her fingers now clasping her bare wrist.

"Let's go look in the car. Maybe it fell off on our way home," suggested Monique.

The girls looked all through the car, but no pink bracelet was found.

"What am I going to do now?" pouted Daisy. "I will never win without my lucky bracelet, and I forgot my lucky rabbit's foot. I want to go home," she wept.

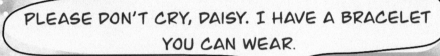

"Please don't cry, Daisy. I have a bracelet you can wear," offered Monique.

"It won't be the same. My sister bought it for my birthday, and she taught me how to make it bring good luck. She told me to put dirt all over it, soak it in alcohol, let it dry for three days, and then say, 'shacka lacka boom boom'. That's why it's so lucky," sobbed Daisy.

"What does luck mean, Daisy?" asked Monique.

"I don't know, but every time I wear my lucky bracelet, good things happen to me. I make good grades on my tests, I always get to be the line leader, and I win the relays at recess," Daisy answered holding up fingers on behalf of each victory.

"Do you know what luck means, Danielle?" asked Monique.

"No, but Grandma always tells us, 'If you don't know what a word means, look it up in the dictionary'," Danielle said with her hands on her waist mimicking Grandma.

"That's a good idea!" said Monique.

The three cousins rushed into the house to find the meaning of the word *luck*.

"Hi, Grandma," they buzzed zooming by the kitchen like three race cars.

"No running in the house, girls," Grandma demanded while stirring her dinner pots.

"Yes, ma'am," the girls replied immediately decreasing their speed to a snail's pace.

"Here is the dictionary I use when doing my homework," said Danielle dropping to the floor sitting criss-cross applesauce.

Turning the pages, "H, I, J, K, L… There it is," said Daisy.

"Lucky charm. An object that is believed to bring good things or events," read Danielle.

"I will never win Red Light, Green Light without my lucky bracelet," whined Daisy.

"Last week, I lost the potato sack race, and everybody was yelling good luck. Does that mean I need a lucky bracelet or a foot too?" Monique questioned the two older cousins.

"I don't think so," said Danielle. "In my Sunday school class, we learned about a boy named Jeremiah, who told the people that God has only good plans for them. So why do we need to be lucky for nice things to happen to us when God has good plans for us?" asked Danielle.

"I don't know," Daisy said shrugging her shoulders.

"And Grandma said, 'God is everywhere'," added Monique placing her hand on Daisy's shoulder.

"I have an idea!" exclaimed Danielle rising from the floor. "Girls, stand and raise your right hand. From this day forward, we will make a pledge to say, 'God bless you' instead of 'Good luck'. God has good plans for us, and we don't need to be lucky for good things to happen," declared Danielle.

"Daisy, you don't need a lucky bracelet or a creepy rabbit's foot. All you need is God's blessing! Last night, the president said, 'God bless America'. He didn't say, 'Good luck America'," suggested Monique.

"I'm not lucky. I'm blessed!" avowed Daisy.

Danielle, Monique, and Daisy raised their right hand, and they all decided to receive and believe in God's blessings and not in luck. Daisy's dimpled cheeks glistened as the three girls zipped out of the house with their hope in God and not in luck.

The two cousins proudly lined up again and Danielle yelled, "On your mark! Get set!"

Daisy cheerfully interrupted once more, "God bless you, Monique!"

"God bless you too, Daisy," Monique said with a huge smile.

"Go, green light!" screamed Danielle.

Daisy and her cousins' summer vacation was off to a great start with God's blessings and no more need for any good luck.

"For I know the plans I have for you," says the Lord. "They are plans for good and not for disaster, to give you a future and a hope." Jer. 29:11 (NLT)

About the Author

Suebrenia Calhoun, a.k.a. Sue, was born and raised in Laurel, Mississippi. At the age of eight years old, Sue's Christmas list consisted of a desk and typewriter. Regardless of her never-ending struggles, Sue's mother financed a walnut wooden desk and a manual typewriter. Purpose was inevitable. Writing and working with this generation are the chromosomal makeup in this author's DNA. Suebrenia has a master's degree in higher education and is an instructor at a college in Florida. Sue's hobbies are vacationing, laughing, shopping and her latest attempted endeavor, snorkeling. Suebrenia's mantra: Words have the power to change you and the world.

Acknowledgements

I would like to express my sincere gratitude to my illustrator, Kaila Richman, an aspiring graphic designer college student. This beautiful young lady was introduced to me by my daughter, Daysia, and we became a match made in heaven. I do not believe in luck and know that Kaila's presence was sent as a gift from God. Kaila's beautiful spirit and youthful encouragement made this long, waited-for labor of love refreshing!